MARVEL

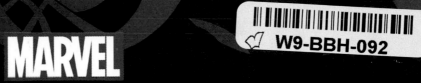

DOCTOR STRANGE

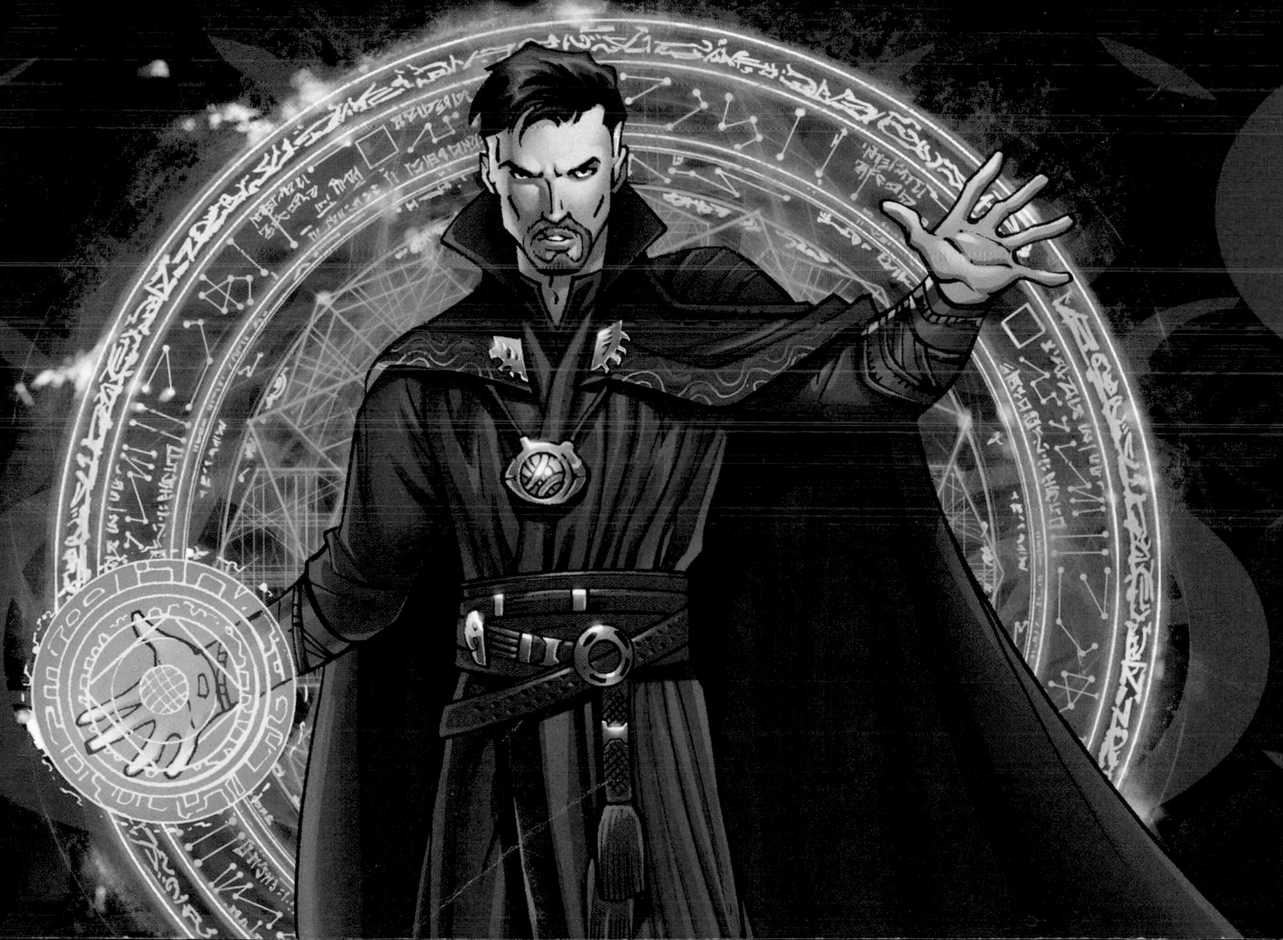

marvelkids.com

Little, Brown and Company

Hachette Book Group
1290 Avenue of the Americas, New York, NY 10104
Visit us at lb-kids.com

Little, Brown and Company is a division of Hachette Book Group, Inc.
The Little, Brown name and logo are trademarks of Hachette Book Group, Inc.

The publisher is not responsible for websites (or their content) that are not owned by the publisher.

First Edition: October 2016

Library of Congress Control Number: 2016949441

ISBN 978-0-316-27185-1

10 9 8 7 6 5 4 3 2 1

CW

Printed in the United States of America

MARVEL

DOCTOR STRANGE

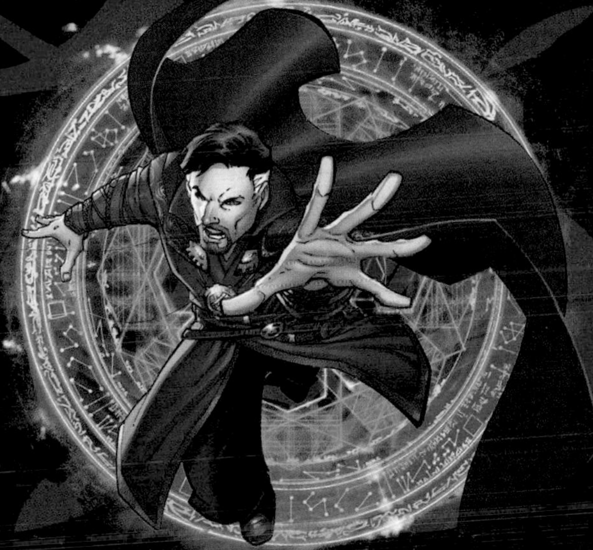

The Sorcerer Supreme

Adapted by Tallulah May
Illustrated by Ron Lim, Andy Smith, and Andy Troy
Based on the Screenplay by Jon Spaihts, Scott Derrickson, C. Robert Cargill
Produced by Kevin Feige
Directed by Scott Derrickson

LB

LITTLE, BROWN AND COMPANY
New York Boston

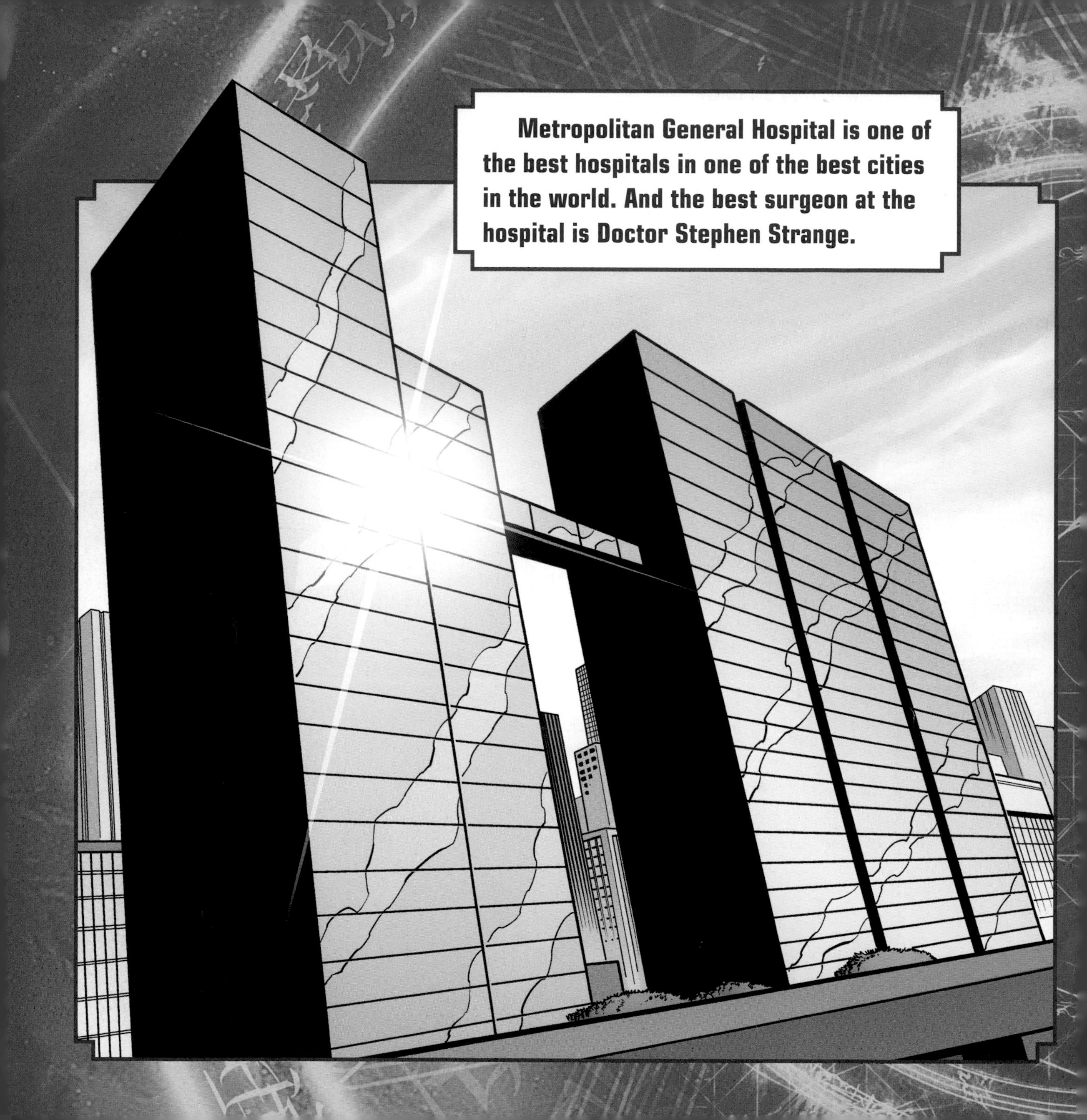
Metropolitan General Hospital is one of the best hospitals in one of the best cities in the world. And the best surgeon at the hospital is Doctor Stephen Strange.

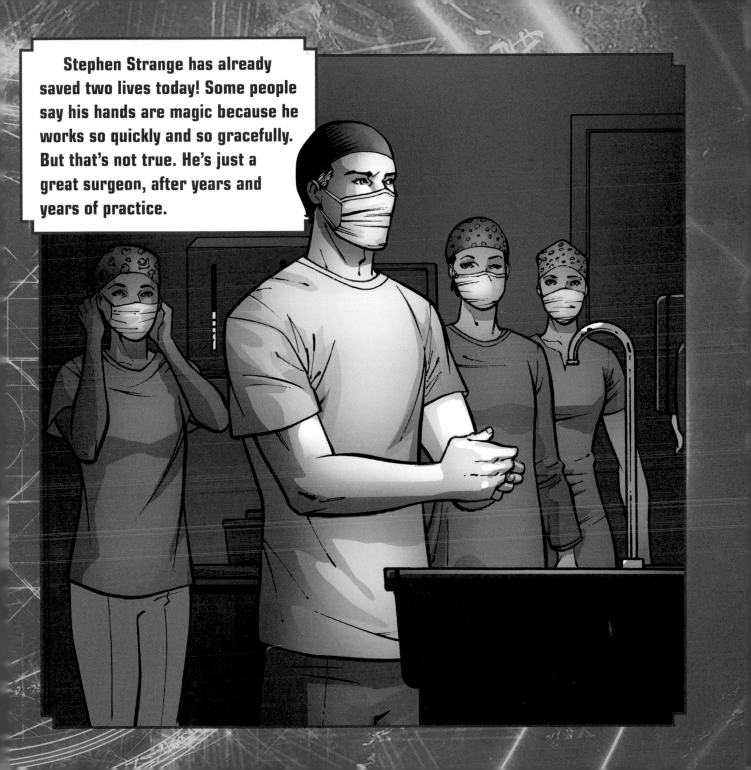

Stephen Strange has already saved two lives today! Some people say his hands are magic because he works so quickly and so gracefully. But that's not true. He's just a great surgeon, after years and years of practice.

When Doctor Strange is finished at the hospital, he puts on his watch and his finest suit. He wants to look his best. Strange always thinks he looks good, but tonight is a special occasion—he is giving an important speech about his work.

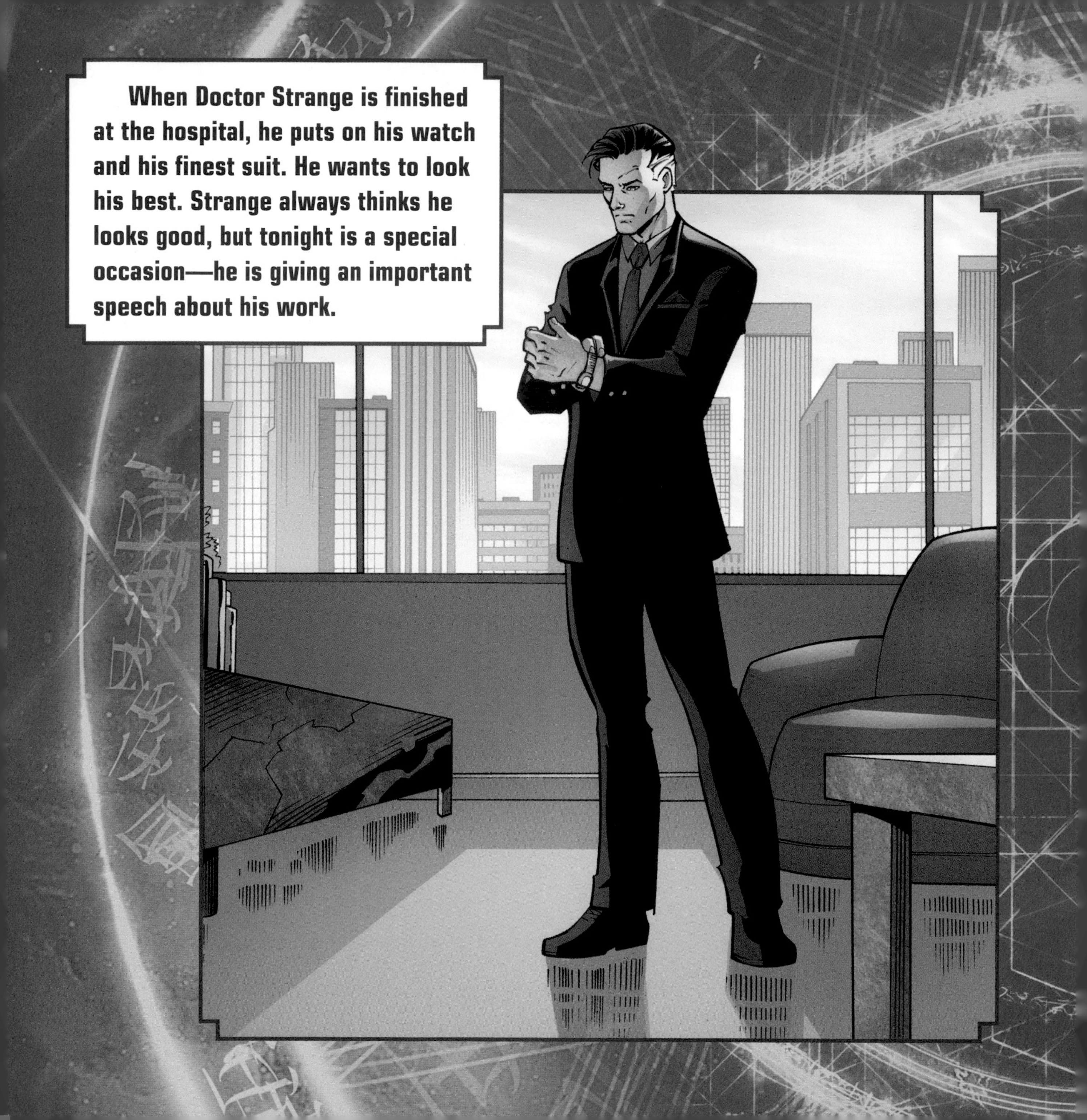

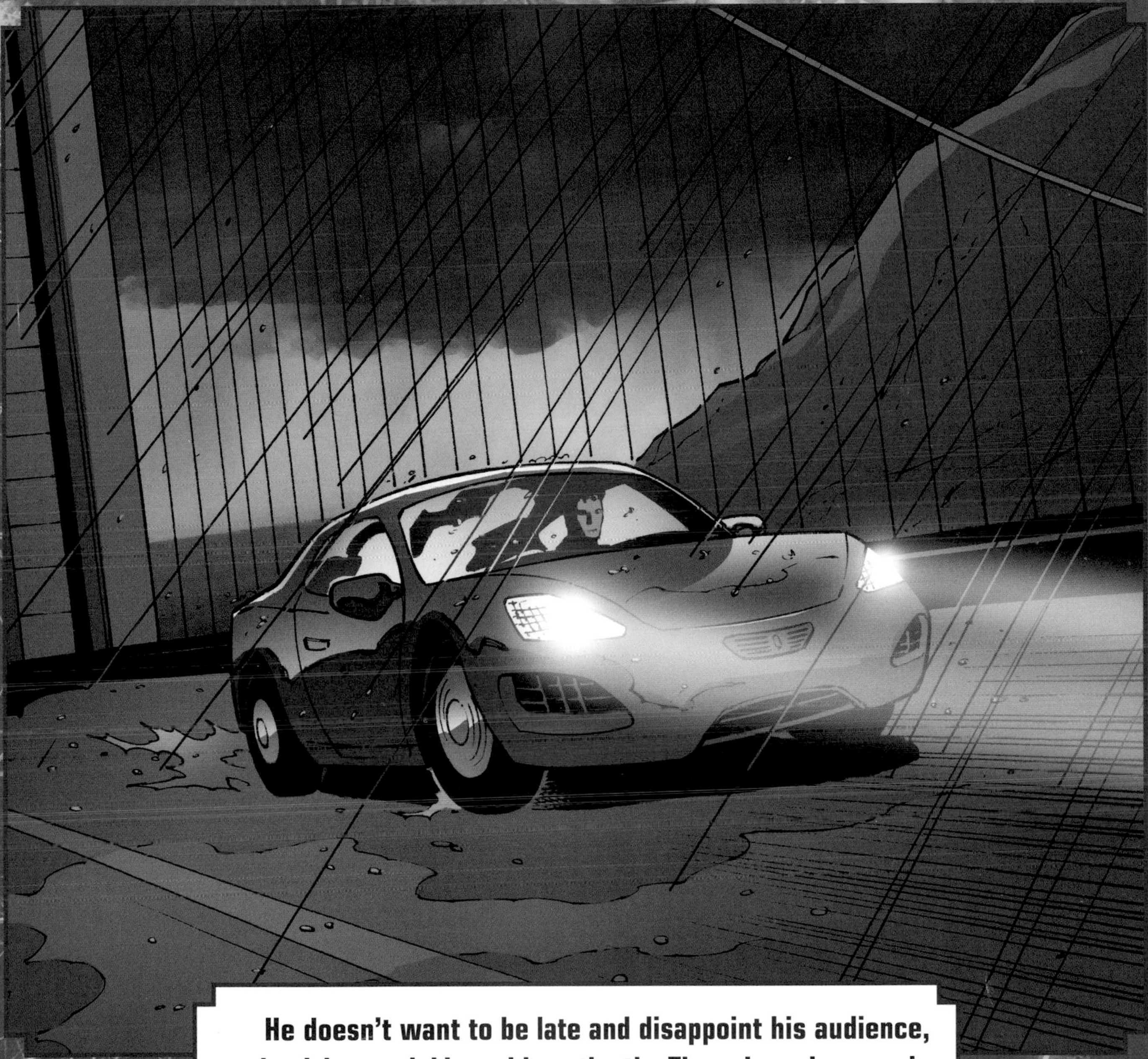

He doesn't want to be late and disappoint his audience, so he drives quickly and impatiently. There is a slow car in front of him, and he is anxious to pass it.

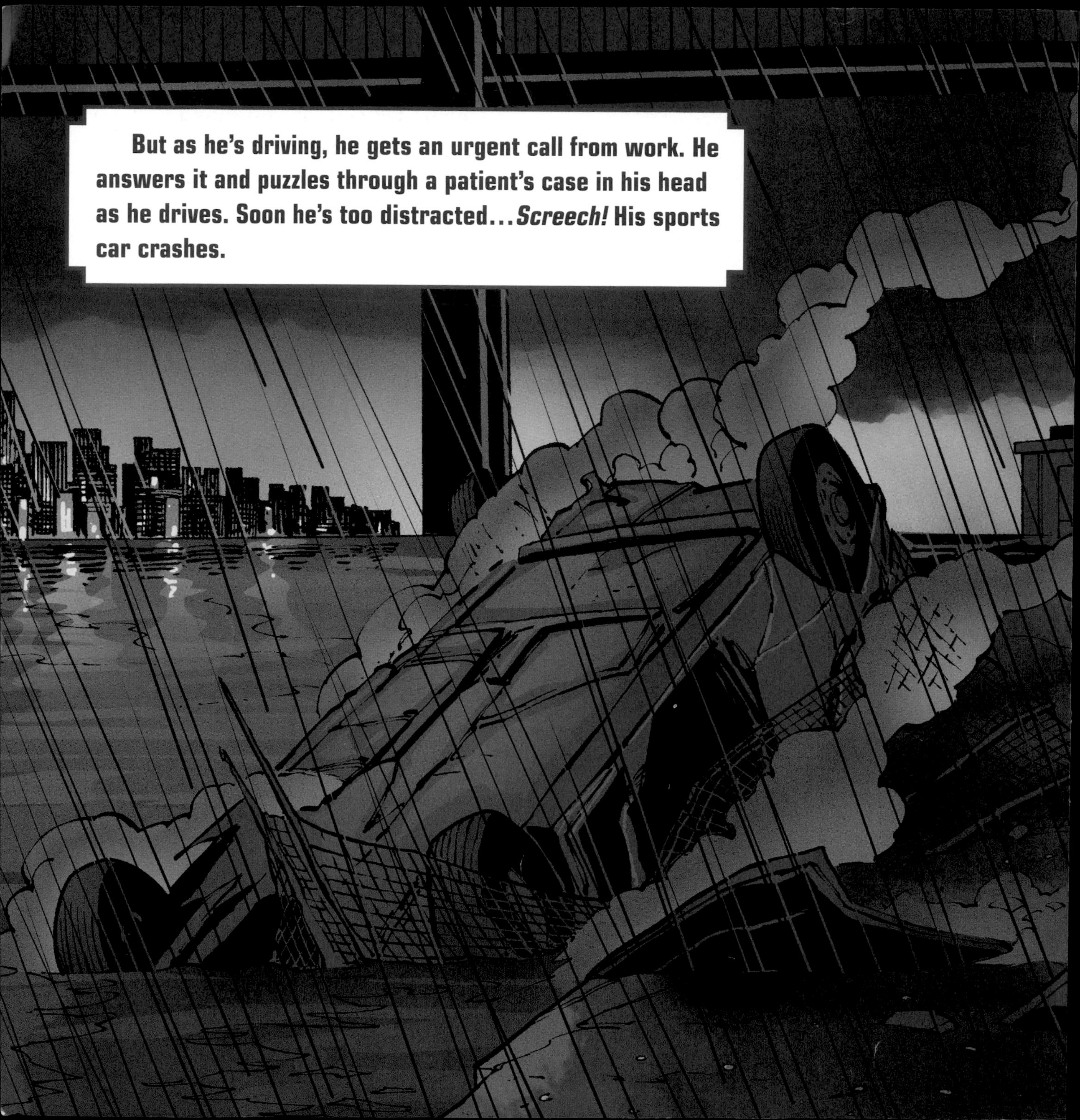
But as he's driving, he gets an urgent call from work. He answers it and puzzles through a patient's case in his head as he drives. Soon he's too distracted... *Screech!* His sports car crashes.

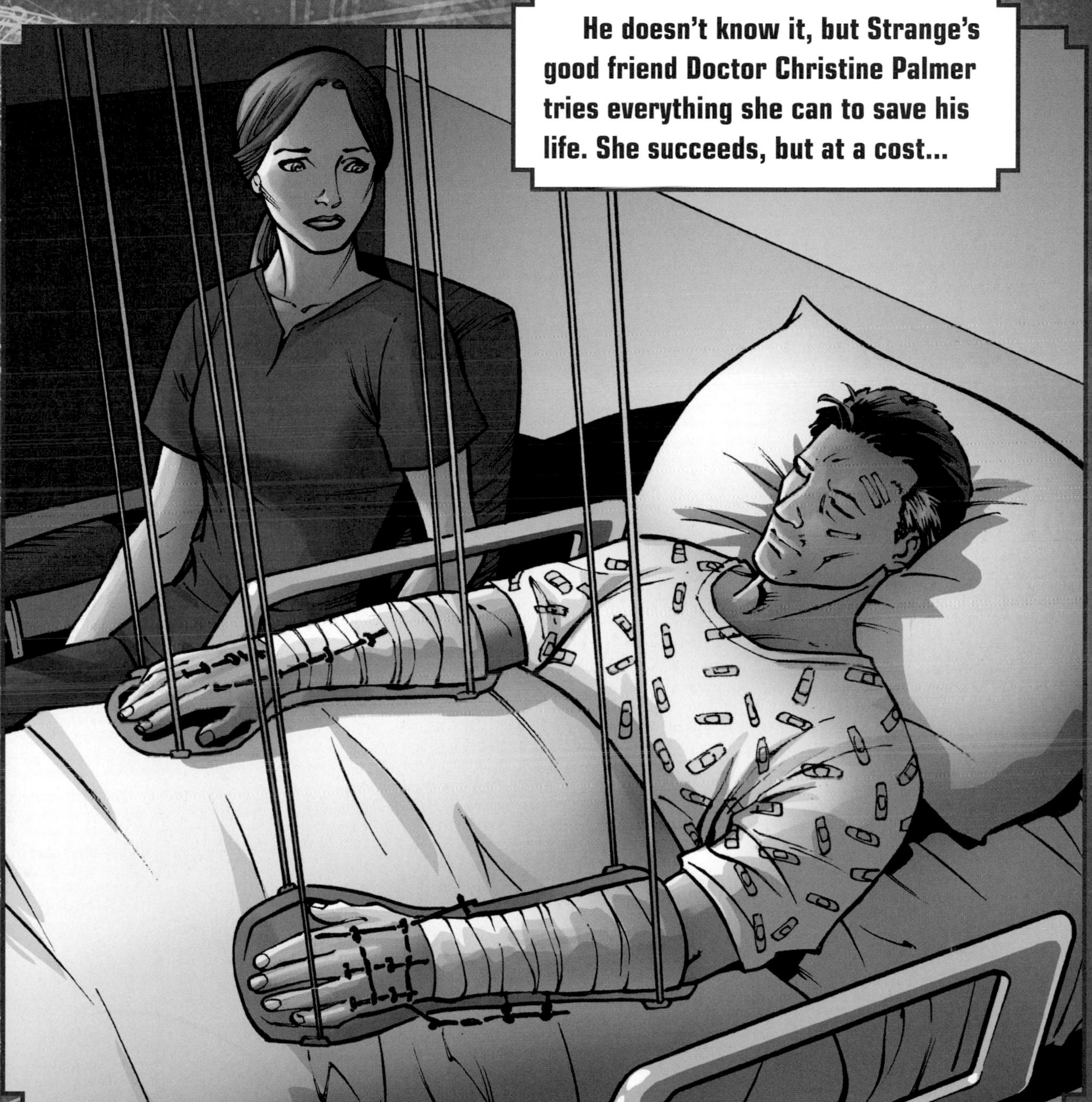
He doesn't know it, but Strange's good friend Doctor Christine Palmer tries everything she can to save his life. She succeeds, but at a cost...

After the accident, Doctor Strange is very upset. His hands are broken, and he can't perform surgery anymore—he is on the verge of giving up hope. There is a rumor of a place that can fix him. It's shrouded in mystery and legend. It's called Kamar-Taj.

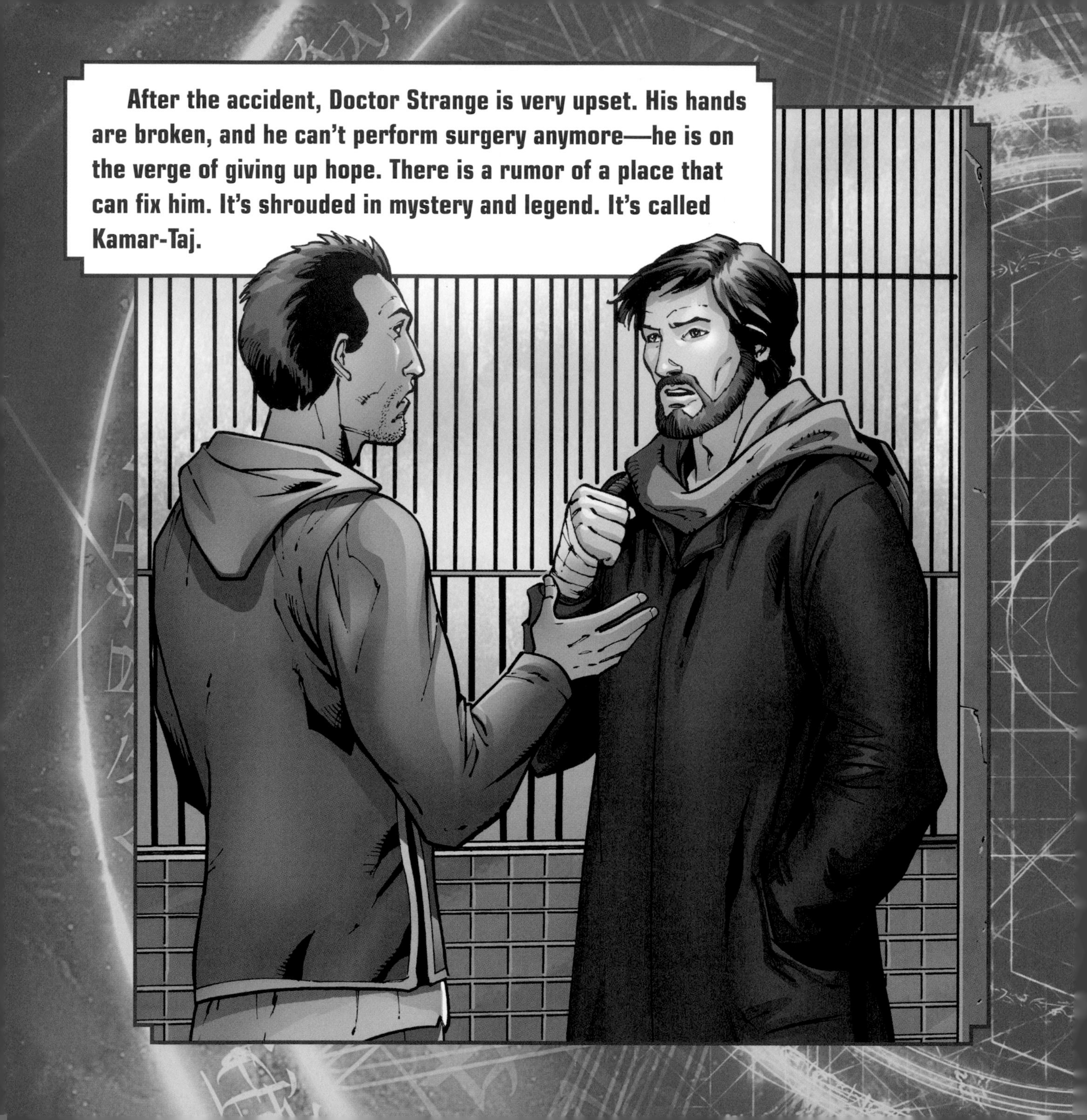

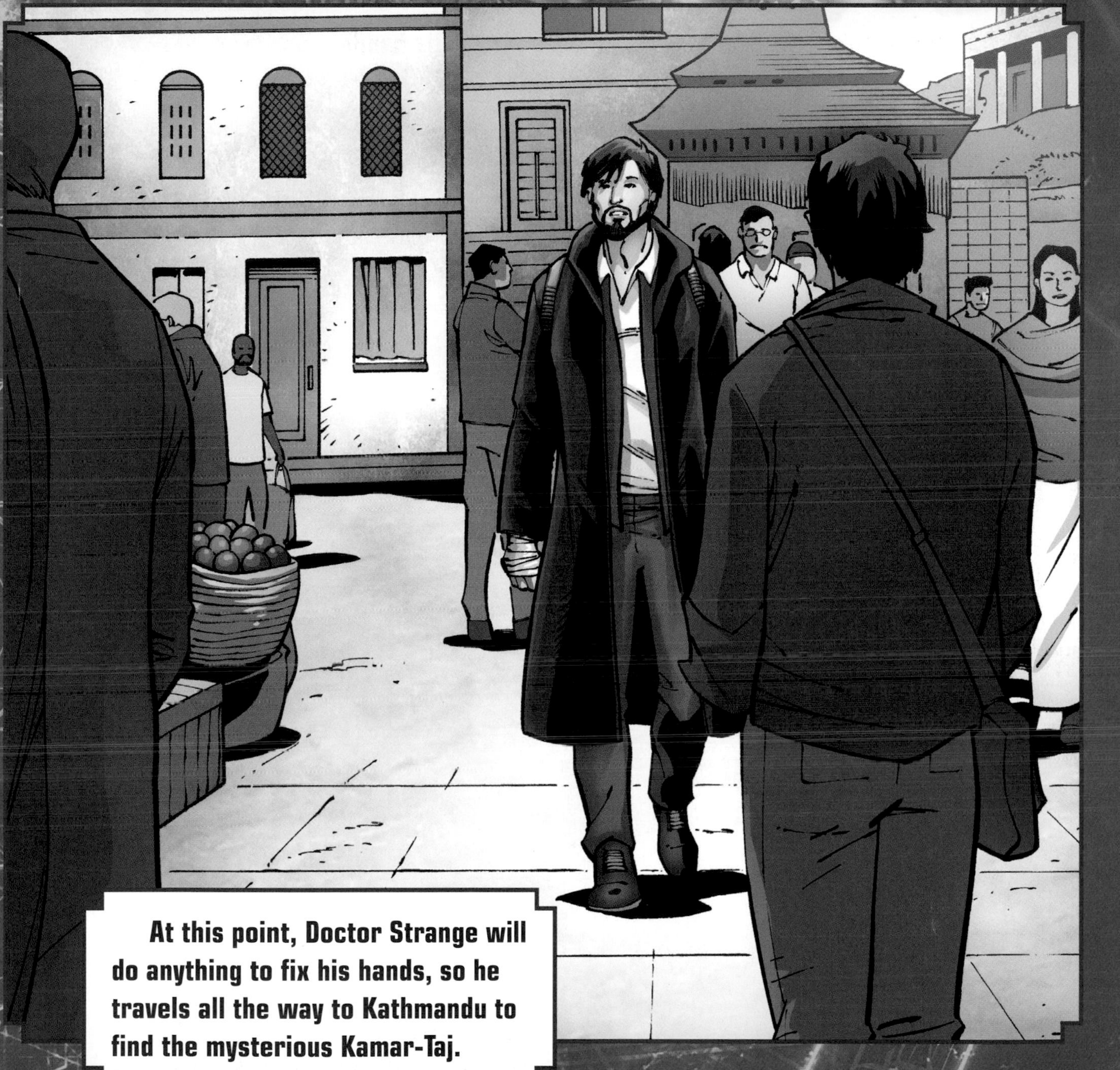
At this point, Doctor Strange will do anything to fix his hands, so he travels all the way to Kathmandu to find the mysterious Kamar-Taj.

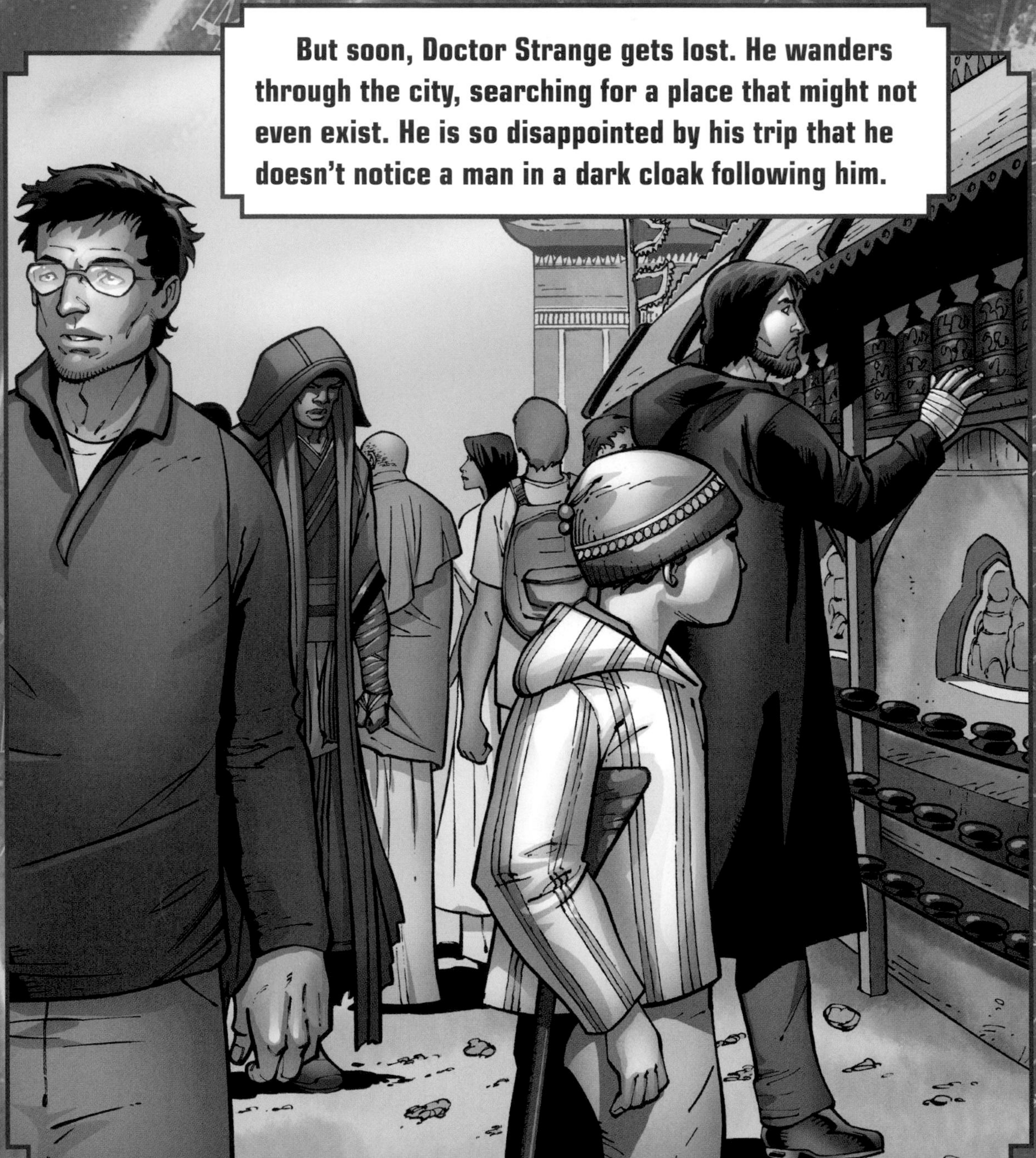
But soon, Doctor Strange gets lost. He wanders through the city, searching for a place that might not even exist. He is so disappointed by his trip that he doesn't notice a man in a dark cloak following him.

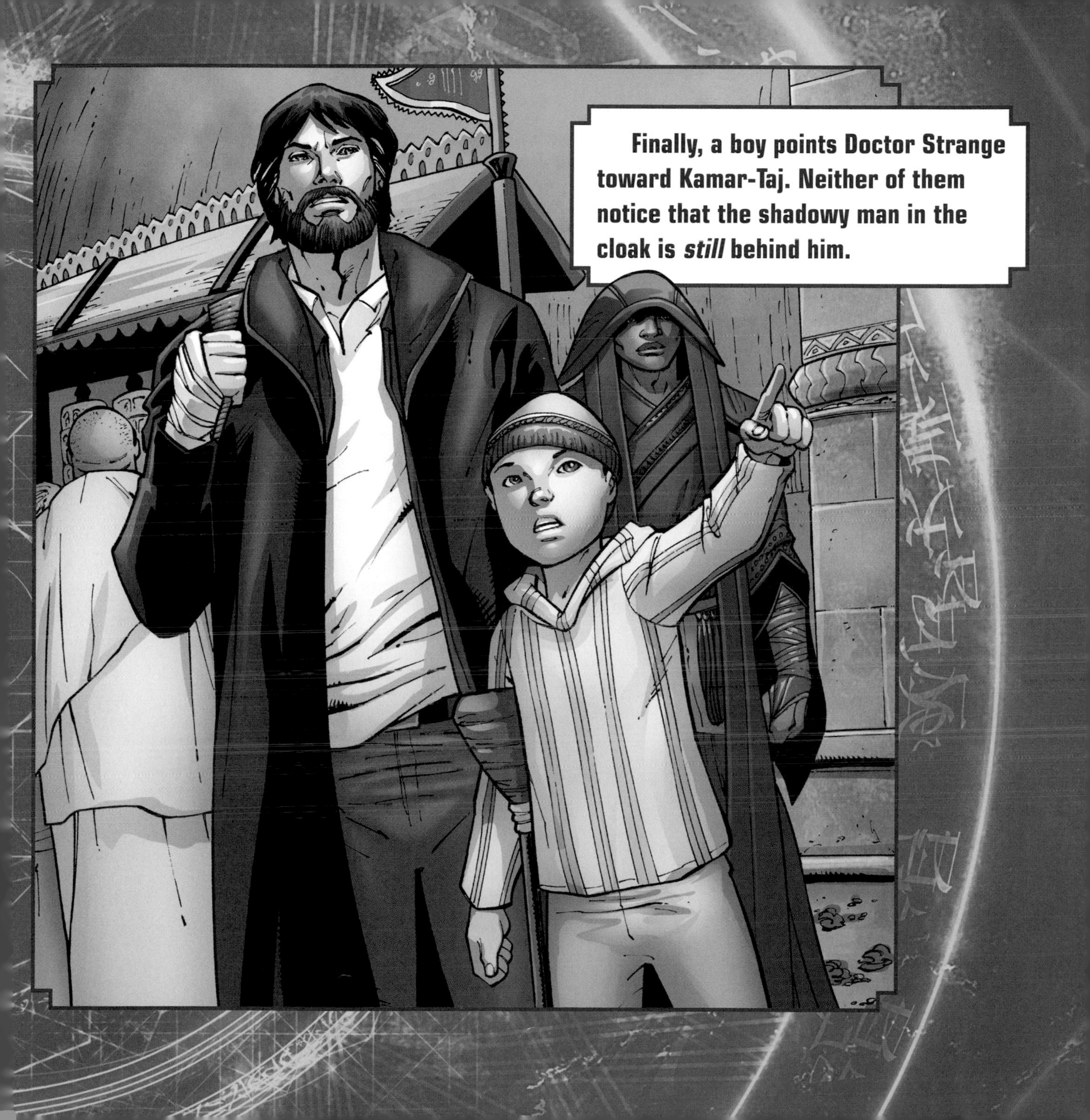
Finally, a boy points Doctor Strange toward Kamar-Taj. Neither of them notice that the shadowy man in the cloak is *still* behind him.

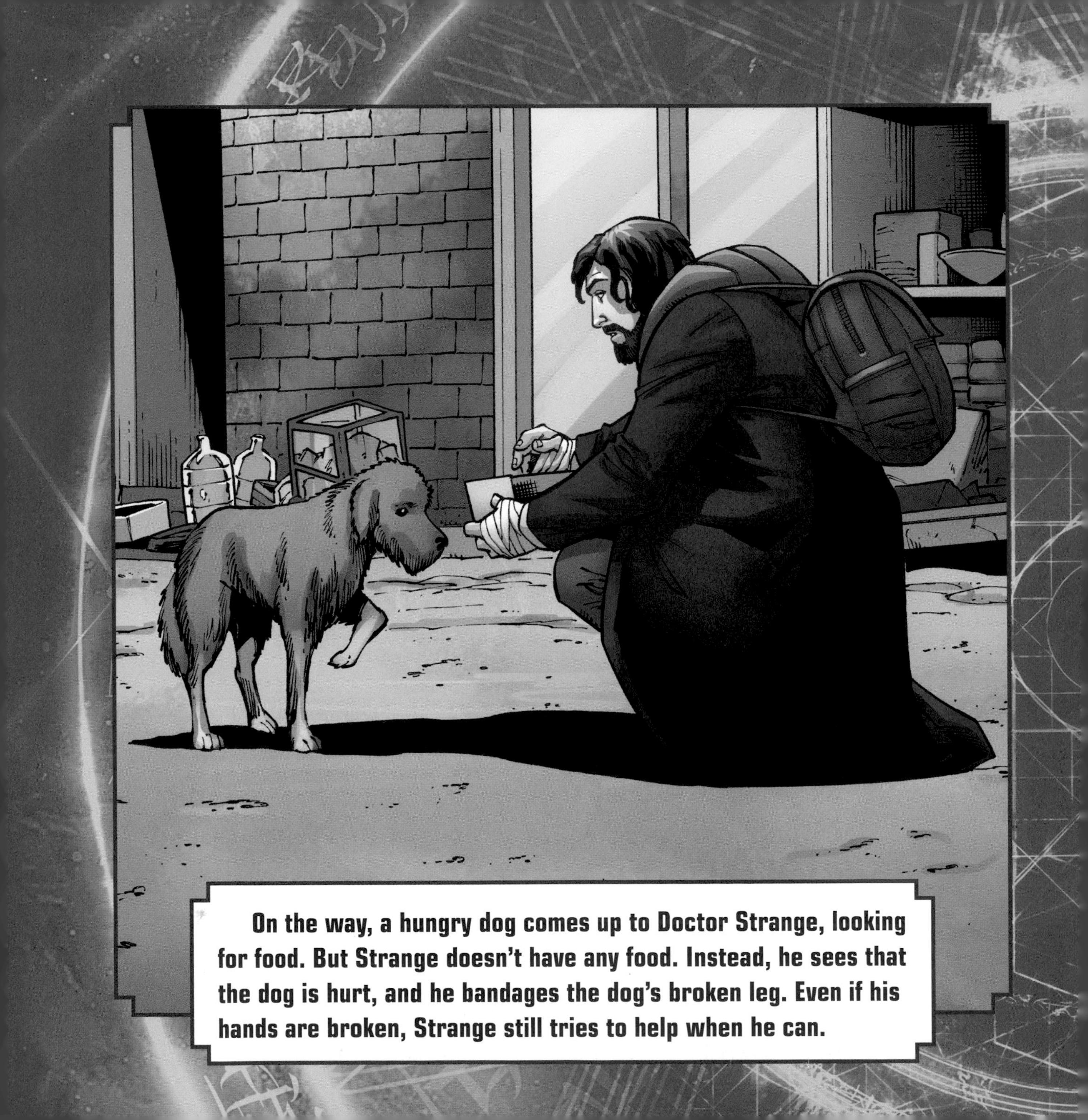

On the way, a hungry dog comes up to Doctor Strange, looking for food. But Strange doesn't have any food. Instead, he sees that the dog is hurt, and he bandages the dog's broken leg. Even if his hands are broken, Strange still tries to help when he can.

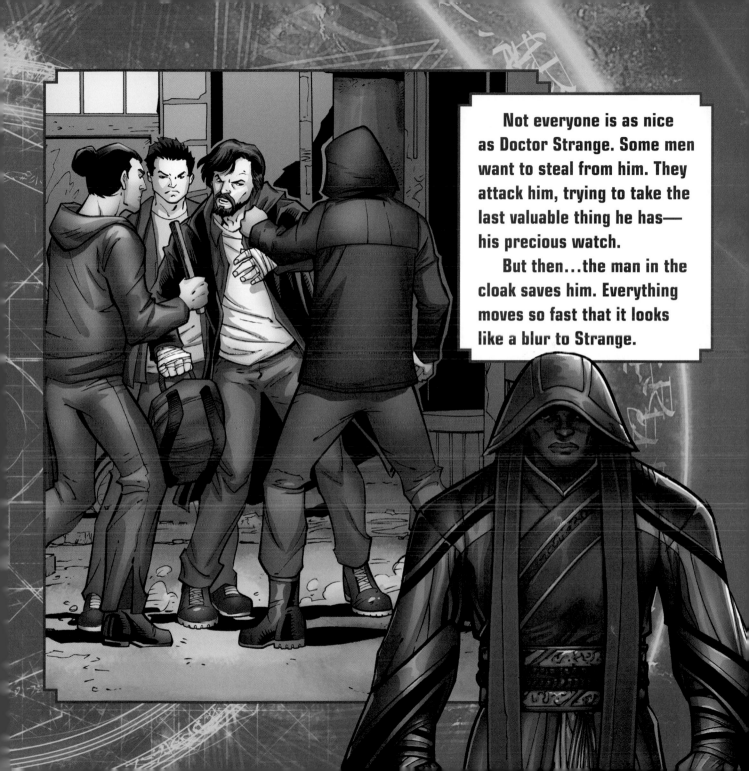

Not everyone is as nice as Doctor Strange. Some men want to steal from him. They attack him, trying to take the last valuable thing he has—his precious watch.

But then...the man in the cloak saves him. Everything moves so fast that it looks like a blur to Strange.

The man in the cloak introduces himself as Mordo and offers to take Strange to Kamar-Taj. Mordo leads Doctor Strange to an unusual building in the middle of the city. It's nothing like Doctor Strange imagined. "You sure you have the right place?" Strange asks.

Mordo stares at him.

"I once stood in your place," the man begins. "And I, too, was disrespectful. So might I offer a piece of advice? Forget everything you think you know."

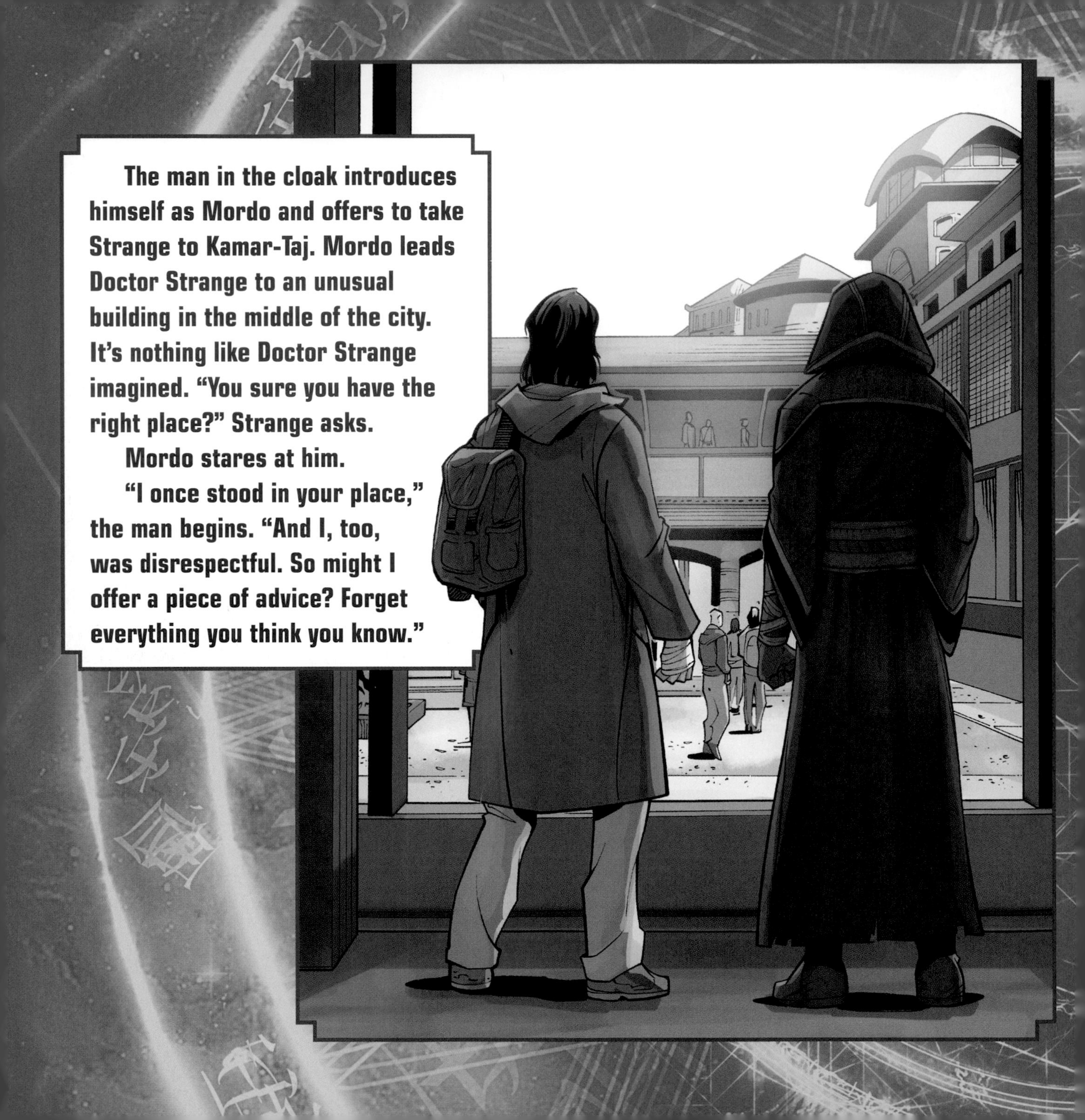

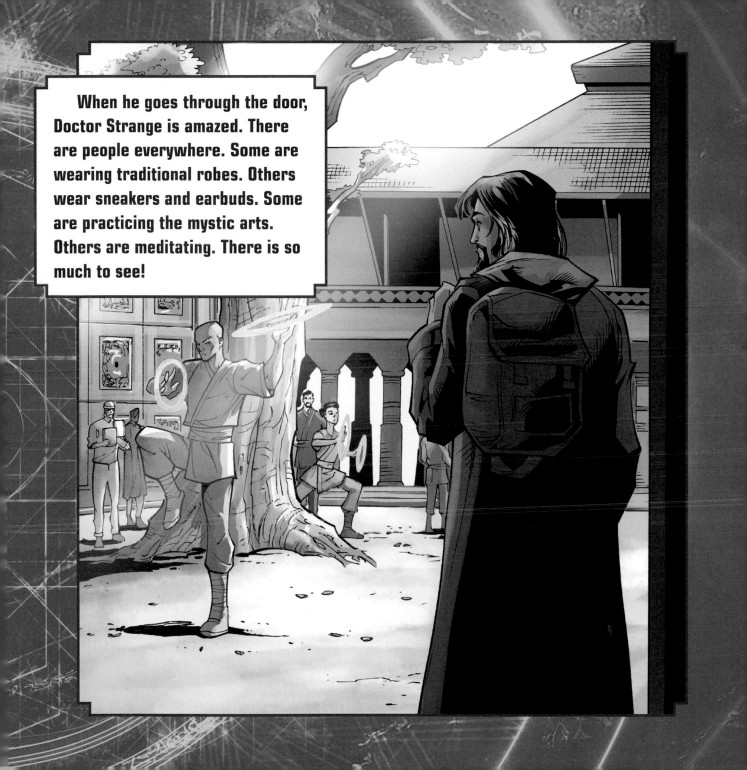

When he goes through the door, Doctor Strange is amazed. There are people everywhere. Some are wearing traditional robes. Others wear sneakers and earbuds. Some are practicing the mystic arts. Others are meditating. There is so much to see!

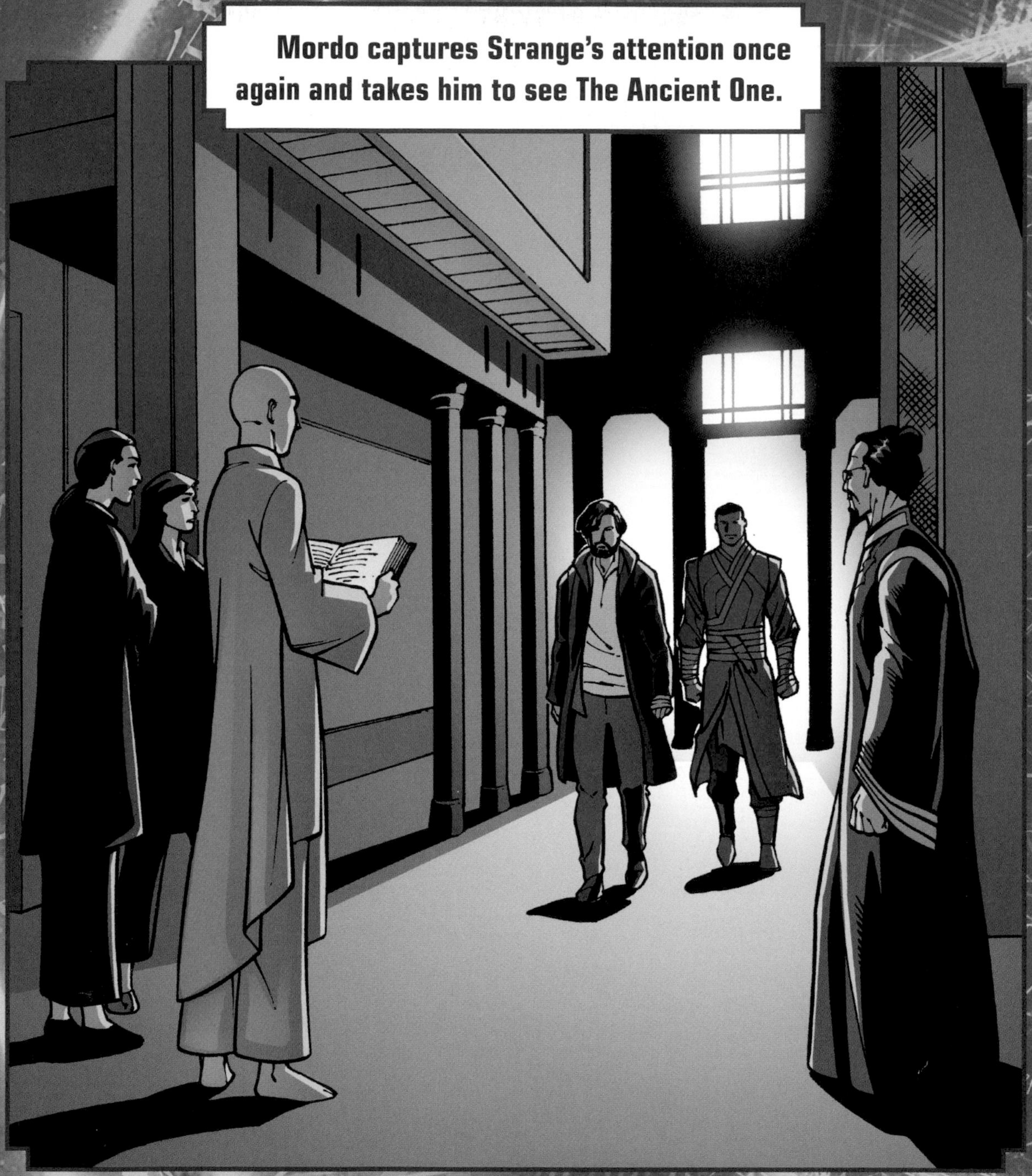
Mordo captures Strange's attention once again and takes him to see The Ancient One.

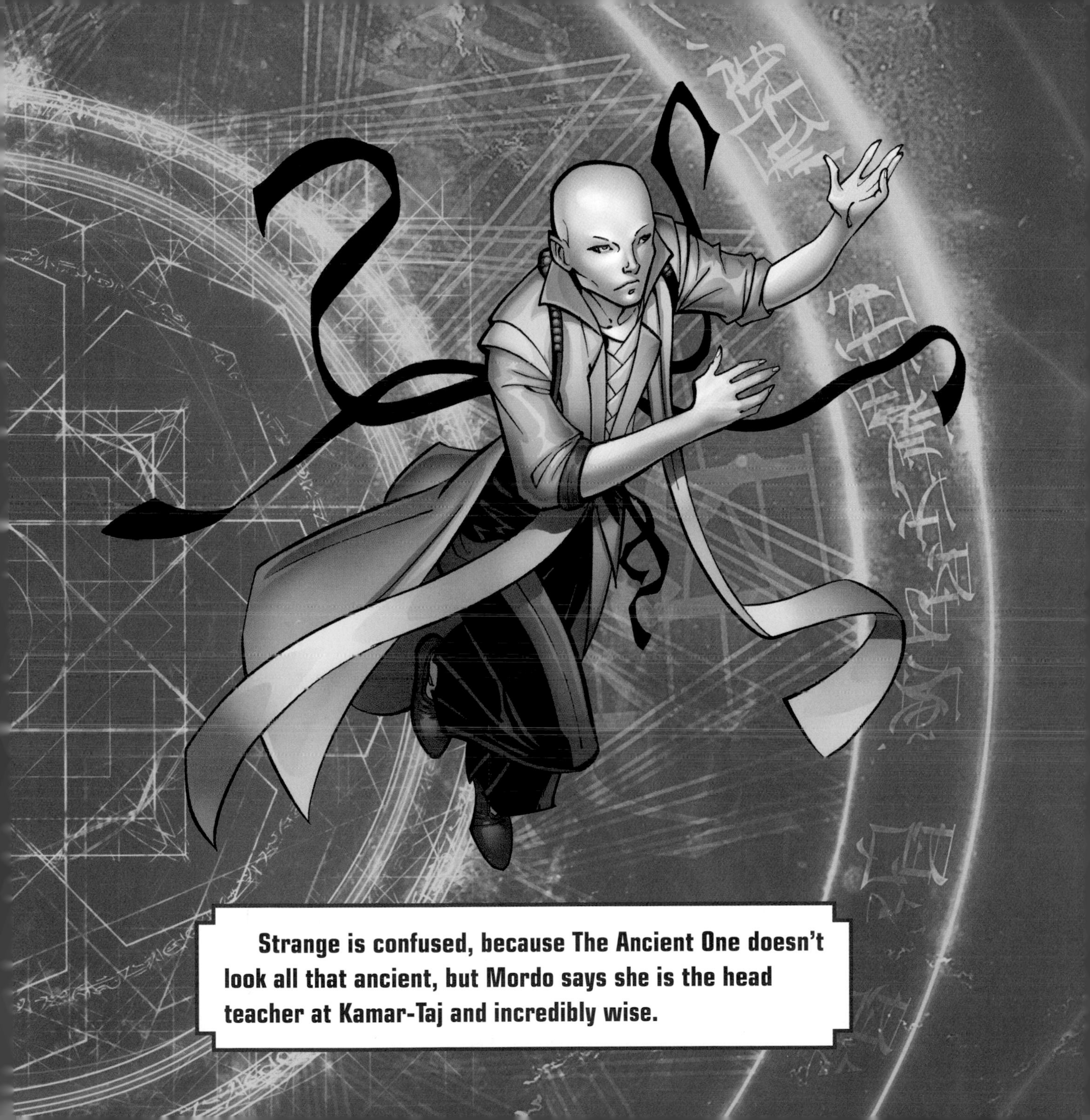

Strange is confused, because The Ancient One doesn't look all that ancient, but Mordo says she is the head teacher at Kamar-Taj and incredibly wise.

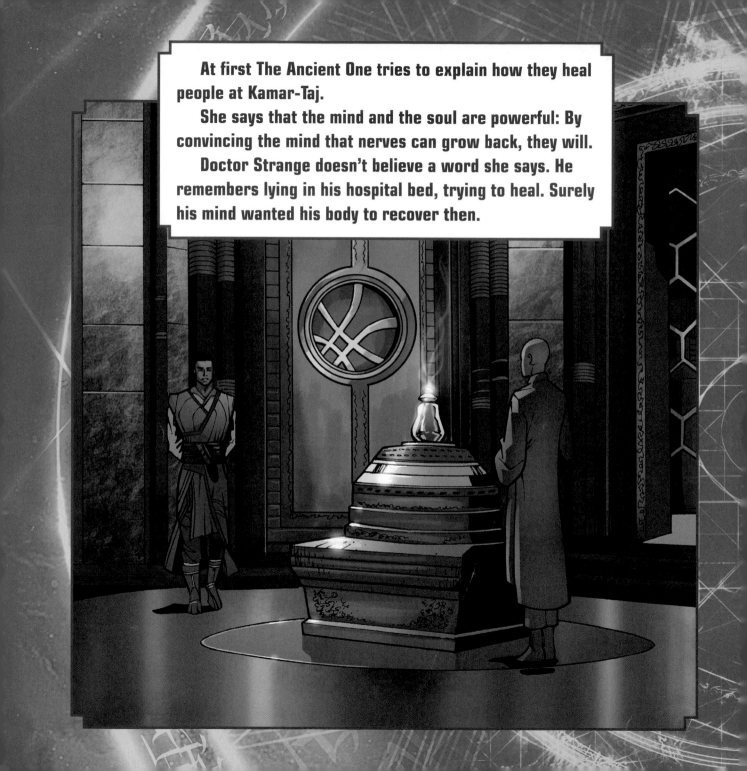

At first The Ancient One tries to explain how they heal people at Kamar-Taj.

She says that the mind and the soul are powerful: By convincing the mind that nerves can grow back, they will.

Doctor Strange doesn't believe a word she says. He remembers lying in his hospital bed, trying to heal. Surely his mind wanted his body to recover then.

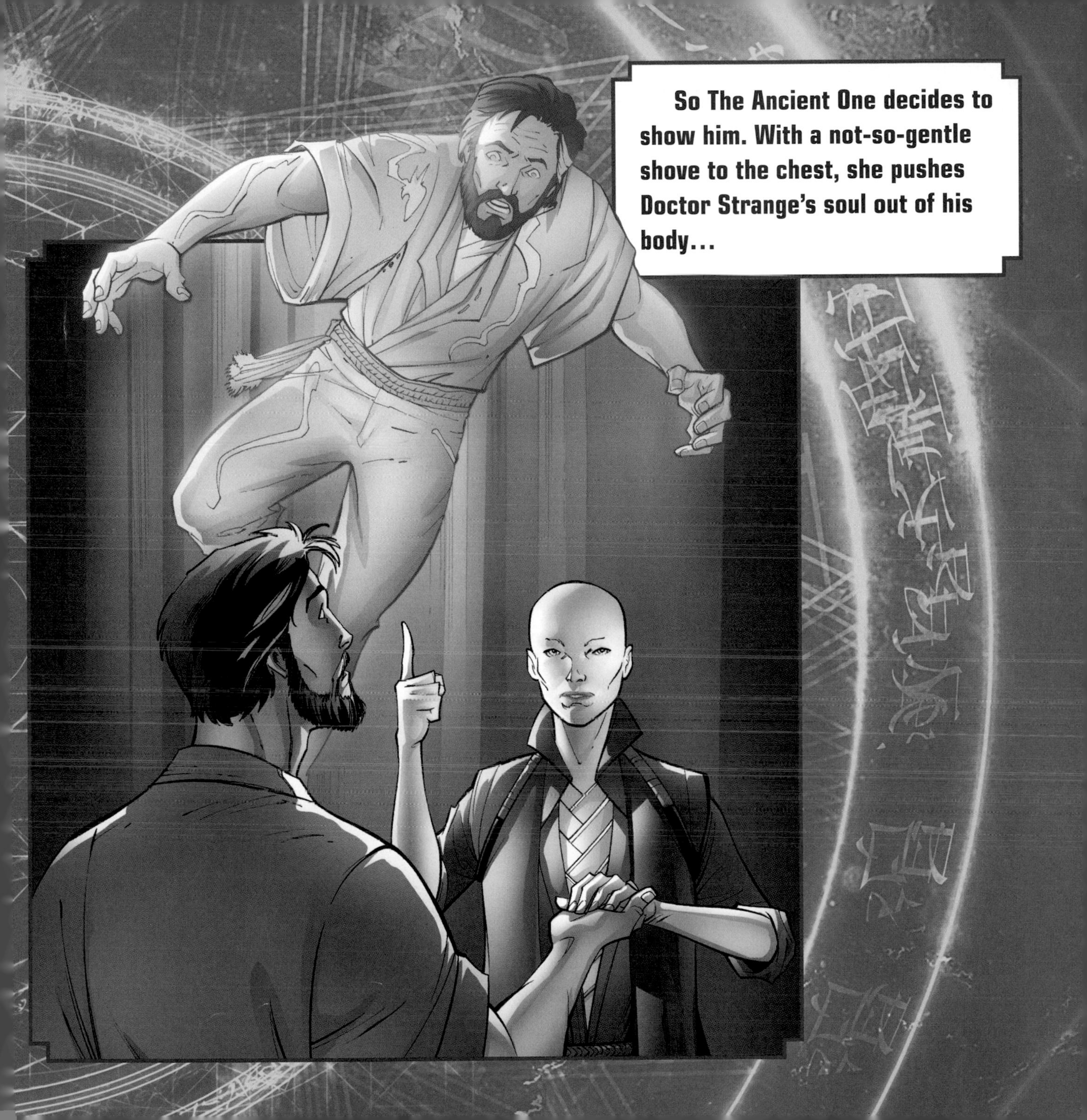
So The Ancient One decides to show him. With a not-so-gentle shove to the chest, she pushes Doctor Strange's soul out of his body…

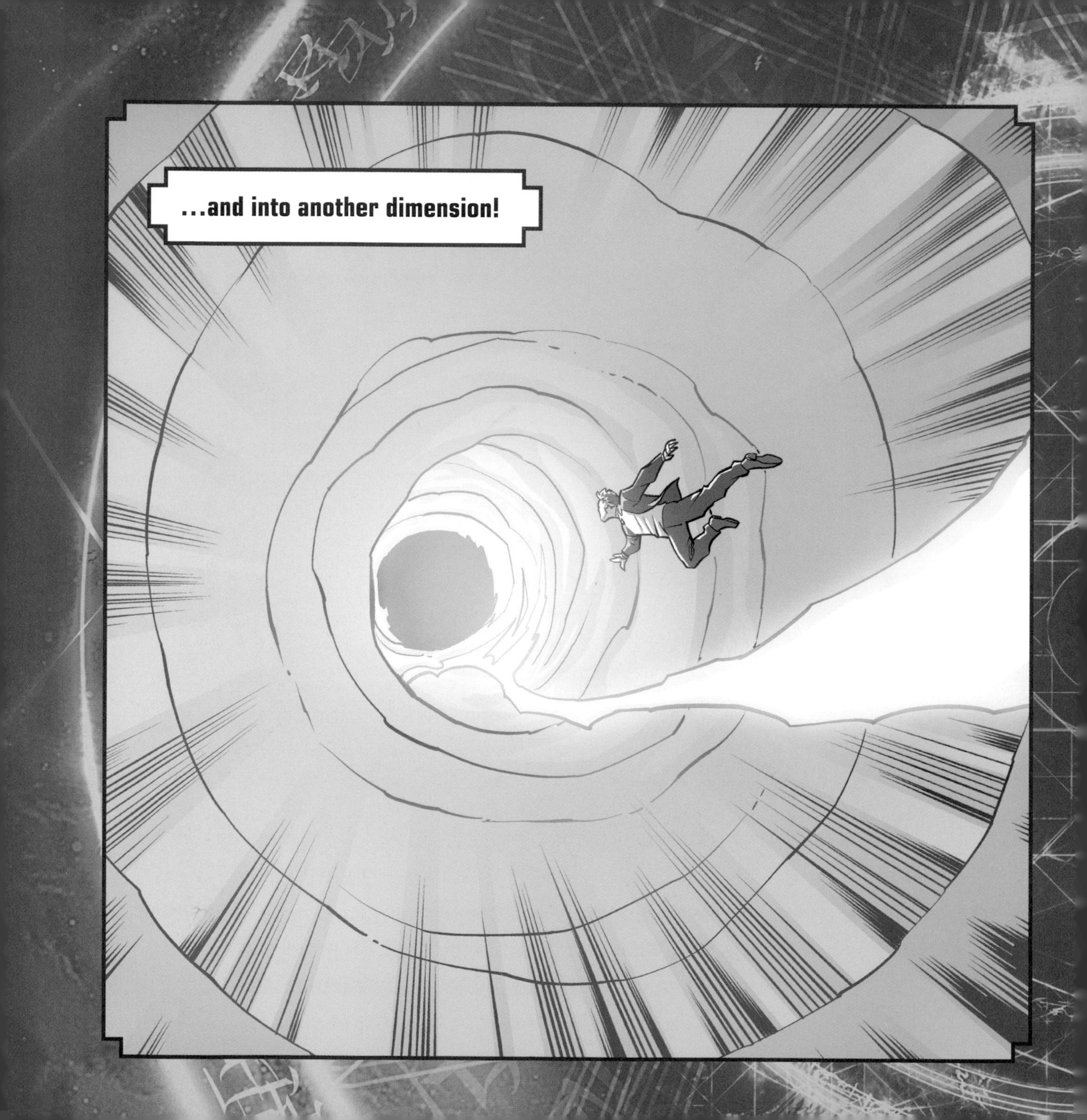
...and into another dimension!

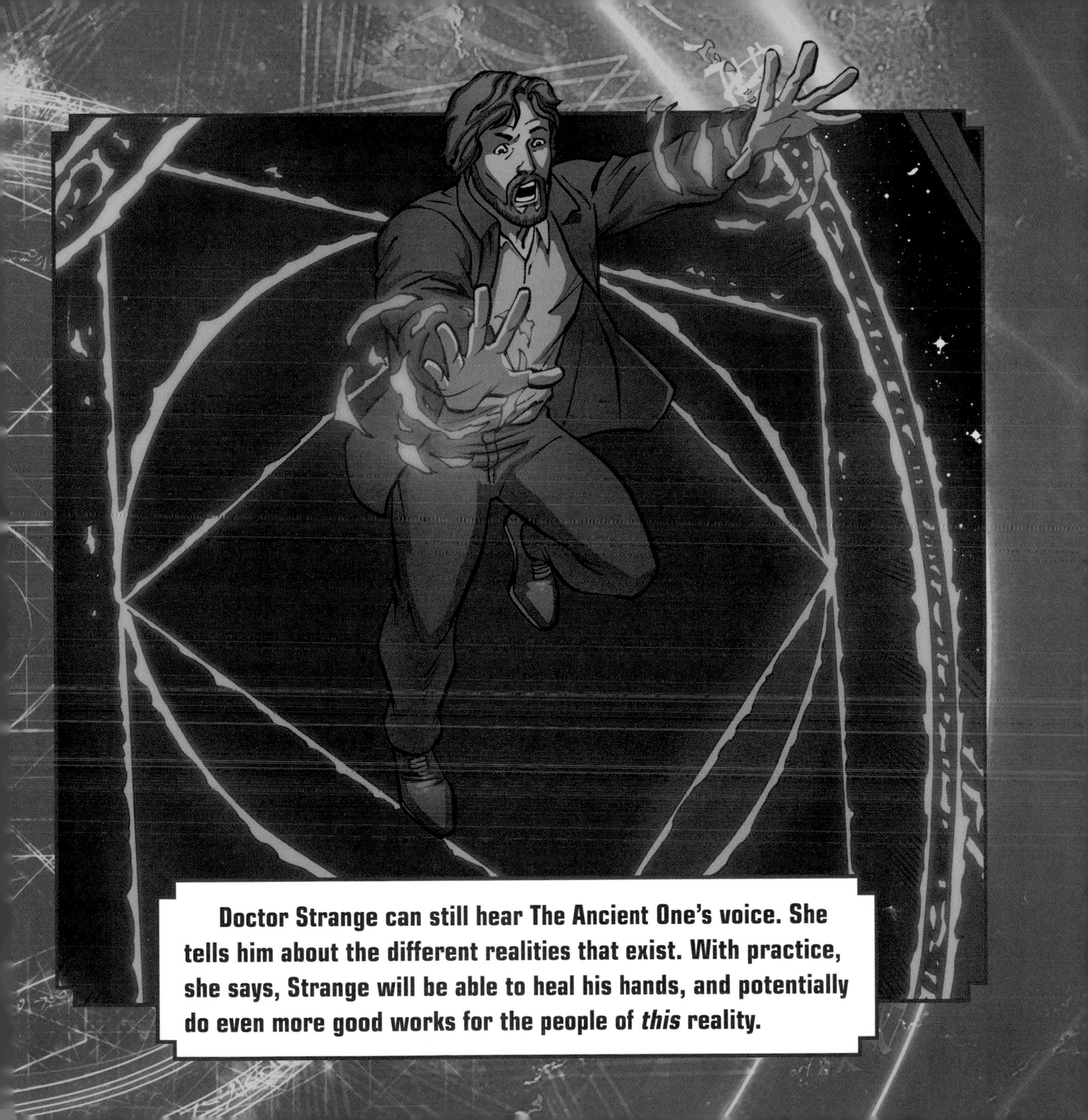

Doctor Strange can still hear The Ancient One's voice. She tells him about the different realities that exist. With practice, she says, Strange will be able to heal his hands, and potentially do even more good works for the people of *this* reality.

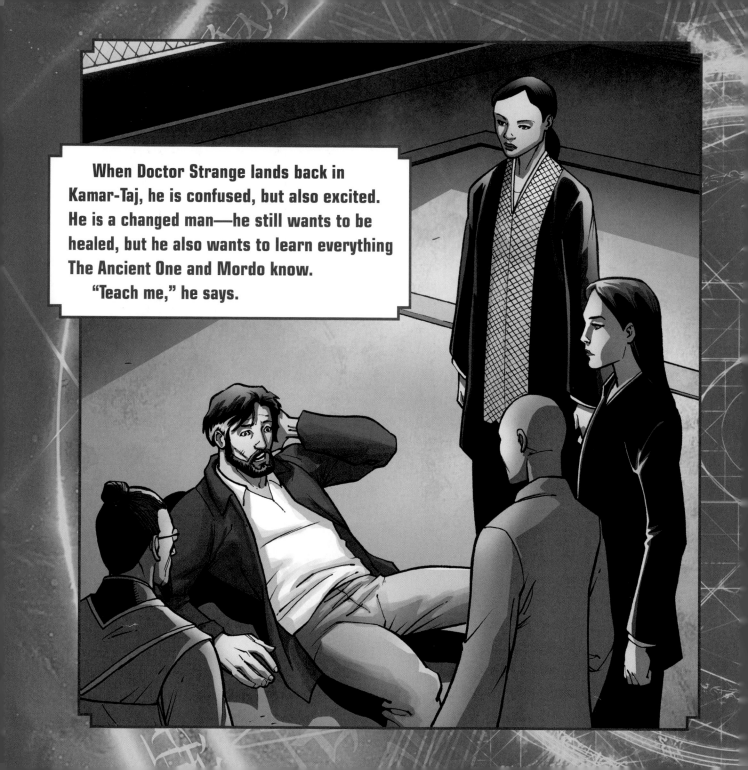

When Doctor Strange lands back in Kamar-Taj, he is confused, but also excited. He is a changed man—he still wants to be healed, but he also wants to learn everything The Ancient One and Mordo know.

"Teach me," he says.